# The Tsunami Quilt

## GRANDFATHER'S STORY

Written by ANTHONY D. FREDERICKS
and Illustrated by TAMMY YEE

*To the memory of Bunji Fujimoto—*
*dedicated community member, respected youth leader, and tsunami survivor.*

TONY

❀

*To the children of Laupāhoehoe—He lei poina 'ole ke keiki—*
*"A lei never forgotten is the beloved child."*

TAMMY

### AUTHOR'S ACKNOWLEDGMENT

Grateful appreciation is extended to Dr. Walt Dudley,
Scientific Advisor for the Pacific Tsunami Museum in Hilo, Hawai'i,
for his continuing friendship, support, and research assistance.

Anthony D. Fredericks

Text Copyright © 2007 Anthony D. Fredericks
Illustration Copyright © 2007 Tammy Yee

Sleeping Bear Press™
310 North Main Street, Suite 300
Chelsea, MI 48118
www.sleepingbearpress.com

THOMSON
GALE

© 2007 Thomson Gale, a part of the Thomson Corporation.

Thomson, Star Logo and Sleeping Bear Press are trademarks
and Gale is a registered trademark used herein under license.

Printed and bound in China.

*First Edition*

10 9 8 7 6 5 4 3 2 1

Library of Congress Cataloging-in-Publication Data

Fredericks, Anthony D.
The tsunami quilt : Grandfather's story / written by
Anthony D. Fredericks ; illustrated by Tammy Yee.
p. cm.
Summary: Once each year, Kimo and his grandfather have placed
a flower lei atop a stone monument at Laupāhoehoe Point, but it
is not until after Grandfather's death that he learns of the 1946
tsunami that took the lives of twenty-four schoolchildren and
teachers, including Grandfather's younger brother.
ISBN 13: 978-1-58536-313-1
ISBN 10: 1-58536-313-8
[1. Grandfathers—Fiction. 2. Memorial rites and ceremonies—
Fiction. 3. Tsunamis—Fiction. 4. Hawaii—History—20th
century—Fiction.] I. Yee, Tammy, ill. II. Title.
PZ7.F872292Tsu 2007
[Fic]—dc22
2006027360

When I was little, my grandfather and I went everywhere, always sharing stories and discovering new places. We were the best of friends.

Each year in the spring, Grandmother would make a beautiful lei of plumeria blossoms. She would give it to Grandfather, placing it gently around his neck. Afterwards he and I would drive to Laupāhoehoe Point. He'd ease his old car down the twisting road to the peninsula and park in the grass near the small cove. Then Grandfather and I would walk along the ocean's edge. We would hold hands and watch the sun dance across the waves.

We never talked much on this
yearly visit. Somehow I knew it was
a time and place for quiet thoughts.

Grandfather always stopped at the marble monument beside the ocean. He would let go of my hand and slowly walk up the stone steps. He would take the lei from around his neck and place it on top of the monument. In silence, he would rest a weathered hand on the stone and stare out over the waves. He would stand there for a long time watching the surf roll in.

Grandfather had been a fisherman all his life. He told me stories of the sea and ancient Hawaiian legends. Every weekend, he and the other fishermen would gather to "talk story" about the ocean. Sometimes I got to listen. The April visit to Laupāhoehoe was the only time I ever saw him so quiet.

"When you are older, Kimo, I will tell you the story of this sacred place," Grandfather promised each year. "You'll learn why it is both a place of tragedy and a place of remembrance. For now, know that the ocean is both friend and foe. It gives, but it also takes."

In those days my family lived in a small house on the Hāmākua coast on the Big Island of Hawai'i. My father was a teacher and my mother was a volunteer at the local school. When my sisters and I weren't at school, we caught fish or swam in the nearby stream.

As a family we laughed and played, and took many trips together. And Grandfather and I were the best of friends.

Then one day my grandfather
was gone. The doctor said it was
a heart attack. My father said it
was a broken heart. It was just after
my ninth birthday and I cried for a
long time. Suddenly I felt all alone.
I didn't understand.

Several days later I went to my father. "Tell me the story of Laupāhoehoe," I pleaded.

My father looked deep into my eyes. There was a sadness in his face as he spoke in a quiet voice.

"I guess you are old enough to know," he began. "Your grandfather would want it so."

"Many years ago, long before you were born, the school was down on the peninsula. The teachers' cottages were along the shore, and all the classroom buildings were arranged around the great spread of a Banyan tree."

"One April morning the rising sun sparkled on the water as it had for thousands of years. As usual, many students came to school early and gathered along the shore. Others were playing on the baseball field. More students were still arriving by bus or walking along the road that snakes down from the cliffs above."

"Was Grandfather one of those students?" I asked.

"Yes. On this morning he sat in the rear of the bus with his younger brother. As the bus rounded a turn in the road, some of the students in the front shouted, 'there's no water in the ocean.' At first your grandfather thought that it was just a joke. But then they repeated, even louder than before, 'there's no water in the ocean!'"

"Your grandfather stood up and looked. He saw that the sea had receded, far beyond the jagged rocks that encircled the tiny peninsula. As soon as the bus stopped, everyone hurried out onto the road and down to the cove. Except your grandfather. Maybe he just had a strange feeling."

"Many students, including Grandfather's younger brother, ran down to the shore. They wanted to see this strange occurrence. Your grandfather watched from a high grassy area some distance behind the wall."

"Then what happened?" I asked.

"Without warning the sea began to swell. Water rose up the shore and onto the road, not in a towering wave, but rather as a powerful surge. It caught everyone by surprise. No one could believe what they were seeing."

"The ocean receded and then rose up again. As before, a wall of water cascaded up the landscape, even higher than before. Some students, including Grandfather, ran farther away from the ocean. Others stayed near the shoreline to see what would happen next."

"The second wave retreated. Then students saw the most terrifying sight of all. It was an enormous wall of water as high as the lighthouse on the point. Suddenly everyone knew — it was the third wave of a tsunami!"

"Was Grandfather scared?" I asked.

"Yes he was, because this wave was dangerous and more powerful than the first two. The wave rushed in from all sides of the tiny peninsula. The ocean churned everywhere like an enormous pot of boiling water."

"Water crashed through the cottages. The buildings were crushed and the wreckage swept out to sea. Boards, branches, and debris were scattered across the peninsula. The wave rose to the height of the coconut trees smashing everything in its way. Teachers and students were swept off their feet and out into the ocean. People were scrambling everywhere, frightened and confused. Everyone was trying to escape."

"What did Grandfather do?" I asked.

"Your grandfather ran up the road to the cliffs with all the power in his legs. He stopped and turned to see people tossed around like dolls. He stared as classmates were sucked into the ocean and beyond the shoreline. He heard their cries and screams."

"Did many people die?"

Father looked at me and reached out to hold my hand.

"Yes, Kimo, the tsunami waves were terrible. The third wave rose more than thirty feet above sea level. It was everywhere. In the end, twenty-four students and teachers were killed."

"Is that the reason for the marble monument by the cove?" I asked.

"Yes. On that monument are etched the names and ages of the children and teachers who lost their lives that day."

"So that is why Grandfather and I visited Laupāhoehoe each year?"

"Yes, Kimo, but there is something more you must know."

My father took me outside. We climbed into his car and headed east toward Hilo. Shortly after crossing the Wailuku River, he turned the car and parked it near a large stone building. As we walked through the door I read the sign—Pacific Tsunami Museum.

Father held my hand tightly as we wound our way through the different exhibits and displays. We stopped in front of a large quilt hanging on the wall. The quilt was in bright colors of blue and yellow. I counted twenty-four squares around the border of the quilt. There was a small wave and a person's name inside each square. In the center of the quilt was an image of a large tsunami wave. Next to the quilt was a sign. I slowly read it aloud:

> *"Students donate quilt to Tsunami Museum out of respect for those who lost their lives at Laupāhoehoe Point during the April 1, 1946 tsunami. Students from Laupāhoehoe Elementary and High School finished this special quilt. The quilt commemorates the twenty-four students and school faculty who lost their lives at Laupāhoehoe Point during the morning of April 1, 1946. The colors of the quilt represent the school's colors: blue and gold. On December 19, 1997 the quilt was donated to the Pacific Tsunami Museum."*

In memory of
those who
lost their
lives in
the

1946 TSUNAMI
AT LAUPAHOEHOE POINT

I watched as Father reached out and gently touched one of the squares. "This is your great-uncle's," he said.

I looked at him, puzzled.

"Your grandfather's younger brother was one of the children swept away by the tsunami that day. Grandfather watched as he was carried out to sea by the third wave. There was nothing he could do. He was frightened and helpless. His brother was your age, nine years old, when he died," he said. "Grandfather felt all alone. He learned to forgive, but he never forgot."

I stared at the quilt and my eyes began to fill with tears. Now I understood.

The next day was April 1. My grandmother made a beautiful lei of plumeria blossoms and placed it gently around my neck. I rode with my father to Laupāhoehoe. He eased the car down the winding road to the peninsula and we parked in the grass near the small cove. In silence, I walked over to the marble monument and up the stone steps. I removed the lei from around my neck and gently placed it on top of the monument. As I did I heard my grandfather's voice, "The ocean is both friend and foe. It gives, but it also takes."

I looked up and watched the gentle surf rolling in from the sea. Then Father and I stood together and watched the sun dance across the waves.

# Author's Note

Laupāhoehoe in Hawaiian means "leaf of lava." This tiny peninsula juts out from the northern edge of the Big Island of Hawai'i. It was formed thousands of years ago from the eruption of Mauna Kea, one of the volcanoes on the island. In the nineteenth and early twentieth centuries a small town was located on this strip of land. Later, when a rail line was built along the coast, many families and businesses moved to the top of the cliffs. A few homes and the school remained on the peninsula.

Tsunami is a Japanese word meaning "great wave in harbor." The word refers to a single wave or a series of waves (sometimes a dozen or more). Some people call them "tidal waves," but they really have little to do with the tides. About 86 percent of all tsunamis are the result of undersea earthquakes. An enormous earthquake off the Aleutian Islands in the North Pacific generated the tsunami that struck Laupāhoehoe on the morning of April 1, 1946.

A tsunami may race across the open sea at more than 500 miles (800 km) per hour! When a tsunami nears shore, the shallowness of the water acts like a brake. Suddenly the speed of a wave may drop from 500 miles (800 km) per hour to 100 miles (160 km) per hour in a few minutes. The water beneath the wave piles up. In a brief moment, a 2-foot (0.5–meter) high wave at sea may be transformed into a 30-foot (9–meter) high wave on the shore. Typically, there are several waves in a row—

a tsunami wave train (at Laupāhoehoe there were three large destructive waves). Later waves in the wave train jam together and build up even higher than the first.

Because of its location in the middle of the Pacific Ocean, Hawai'i is at risk from tsunamis from all directions. Today the Tsunami Warning System, located on the island of O'ahu, provides valuable information to authorities and residents about earthquake-generated tsunamis. A "tsunami watch" is declared whenever a strong earthquake occurs in the Pacific Basin. A "tsunami warning" is issued to let people know that a tsunami is approaching and that they should move to a safe place.

Tsunamis can occur at any time of the day or any time of the year. They are swift and silent, dangerous and deadly, and memorable for many years after their passage.

The Pacific Tsunami Museum in Hilo, Hawai'i preserves the stories of tsunami survivors. It also has mementos of those who lost their lives in past tsunamis. Included are film and video presentations, computer simulations and virtual reality programs, a children's center, an exhibit on the myths and legends of tsunamis, and public safety programs for visitors and residents alike. One of the most touching exhibits details the events at Laupāhoehoe School during and after the tsunami of April 1, 1946. It includes The Tsunami Quilt.